**DRE**

HOW TO TRAIN YOUR
DRAGON™

HarperFestival is an imprint of HarperCollins Publishers.

How to Train Your Dragon: The Chapter Book
How to Train Your Dragon ™ & © 2010 DreamWorks Animation, L.L.C.
Printed in the United States of America. All rights reserved.
No part of this book may be used or reproduced in any manner
whatsoever without written permission except in the case of brief
quotations embodied in critical articles and reviews.
For information, address HarperCollins Children's Books, a division of
HarperCollins Publishers, 10 East 53rd Street, New York, NY 10022.
www.harpercollinschildrens.com
Library of Congress Cataloging-in-Publication Data is available.
ISBN 978-0-06-156737-7
Book design by John Sazaklis
10 11 12 13 14   LP/CW   10 9 8 7
❖
First Edition

DREAMWORKS

HOW TO TRAIN YOUR
DRAGON
™

THE CHAPTER BOOK

ADAPTED BY J. E. BRIGHT

HARPER FESTIVAL
An Imprint of HarperCollinsPublishers

CHAPTER ONE

My name is Hiccup. I live on an island called Berk. It's a spiky chunk of rock jutting out of the churning ocean. Our Viking village is nestled in a valley between cliffs where green hills roll to the jagged shore.

Berk has good fishing down by the docks, good hunting in the forest, and a great view of sunsets. Our fields are dotted with white sheep.

The only problem is the pests. We have *dragons*.

Tonight, I gulp as I see a pair of claws snatch a sheep. I run out the door and leap off our front porch. Neighbors charge out of nearby buildings, ready to fight.

When faced with constant dragon attacks, most people would leave. Not us Vikings. We're stubborn.

The dragons swoop to grab sheep, or blast our rooftops with their fiery breath. Huge Vikings charge by me, brandishing axes. I dart through an alley, creeping under overhanging eaves, heading toward a safe spot to view the battle. The alley ends at the marketplace near the docks. In the moonlight, I see the shadowy shapes of dragons dodging airborne axes.

My dad, Stoick the Vast, strides into the marketplace. He's our chief, and the biggest Viking alive. They say when he was a baby he popped a dragon's head clean off its shoulders.

I jump back as a dragon spews a fireball, which explodes against a shed. Dad stands firm. He brushes ash off his shoulder, then turns and picks up a wagon. He hurls it at a dragon, which

drops a sheep. Dad
catches it in his arms.

Creeping out of the
alley, I listen as Dad barks at
his men, "What have we got?"

"Gronckles," one Viking replies,
pointing up at a fat gray dragon. "Deadly Nadders
and Hideous Zipplebacks." He waves at a slim blue
dragon and a green two-headed beast. "Johannes saw
a Monstrous Nightmare."

"Any Night Furies?" demands Dad.

The man shakes his head. "Not so far."

"Good," Dad replies. "Hoist the torches!"

The warriors light large braziers, which they
raise on poles. The firelight reveals dozens of dragons
circling overhead. When Dad leads other Vikings
toward the dock, I hurry into the marketplace and
duck into the blacksmith's shop.

The shop is filled with Vikings demanding
weapons. In the back, by the forge near an open wall,

is Gobber—a peg-legged, one-armed meathead with a bad attitude. I've been his apprentice since I was little. Well . . . *littler*.

"Nice of you to join me," Gobber grumbles. "I thought you'd been carried off."

I drop damaged weapons on a table. "I'm too muscular for their taste," I joke, striking a bodybuilder pose. "They wouldn't know what to do with all *this*."

Gobber raises an eyebrow. "They need toothpicks, don't they?"

Through the open wall, I hear Dad hollering. "Move to the lower defenses!" he bellows. "Counterattack with the catapults!"

A sudden burst of flame makes Gobber and me glance outside. Two hefty Gronckles dive-bomb down, coughing slugs of molten lava. The blasts explode a house.

"Fire!" Gobber hollers.

The fire brigade is five teenagers pulling a wooden cask on wheels. They dip buckets into the cask and fling water on the burning building. I know them well. Ruffnut and Tuffnut are twins. Tuffnut is a guy and Ruffnut is a girl, though it's hard to tell from their grungy outfits and equally tough attitudes.

Supporting the cask is Fishlegs, a huge guy with a fringe of blond hair. Dipping buckets is Snotlout, a dark-haired bruiser. And handing buckets to Tuffnut is . . .

Astrid. Sigh. She's the cutest girl in the village.

I hear Gobber's wooden leg as he clomps behind me.

"I need to get out there," I plead.

Gobber shakes his head. "You can't swing an axe, and you can't even throw one of these!" He picks up a bola, two iron balls connected by a rope.

I yank a tarp off my newest invention, which looks like a combination of a wheelbarrow and a catapult. "*This* will throw it for me! I call it the Mangler."

Gobber covers the Mangler. "If you ever want to fight dragons, you've got to stop being *you*."

Killing a dragon is everything around here. A Nadder head will definitely get me noticed. Gronckles are tough—taking one of those down is serious danger. A Zippleback? Two heads, twice the status. And then there's the Monstrous Nightmare. Only the biggest Vikings go after these. They have this nasty habit of setting themselves on fire. . . .

A moaning sound echoes through the night. That's the sound of the dragon we fear most, but have never seen.

"The Night Fury!" Gobber yells.

The Vikings duck. On my knees, I peer around the wall.

The main catapult explodes in a huge fireball. Dad and his men leap away.

Gobber grabs an axe. "Stay put, Hiccup," he orders.

As soon as he's gone, I uncover the Mangler and

push it outside.

Keeping to alleyways, I wheel the Mangler up a slope to a cliff. Below me, I see the Western Catapult, which the Night Fury is sure to target next. I load the Mangler with a bola and aim it at the dark sky.

I hear the eerie whine of the Night Fury. The black dragon is invisible in the night, but I know it's close.

When the Night Fury spews a fireball, the flash reveals its silhouette. I pull the trigger as the Western Catapult explodes. The bola whirls into the darkness.

The Night Fury screeches.

"I hit it!" I cheer. "Did anyone see that?"

My celebration only lasts a second. A huge, red, reptilian head rises over the cliff. I look into the eyes of a Monstrous Nightmare.

"Besides you?" I turn and run.

The Nightmare swoops after me as I barrel down the hill. I zoom past Dad and a few other Vikings who used their fishing nets to capture a bunch of Nadders. "Help!" I scream.

I dodge when I hear the Nightmare cough behind me. It blasts out sticky fire, missing me but hitting a building with lava-like goo. In the plaza, there's nowhere to hide except behind a metal bin. The Monstrous Nightmare belches more sticky flame. The bin protects me, barely.

The plaza falls quiet. I peer around. There's no sign of the Nightmare. I stand up—and see the dragon standing behind me.

Before the Nightmare can broil me, Dad tackles it to the ground. The dragon breaks free and rears up to toast Dad. But it only coughs up smoke.

Dad grins. "You're all out." He smashes the Nightmare's face with his fist. Dad's fury forces the dragon back, until it flies away.

The bin's burnt pedestal collapses. The bin rolls across the plaza, picking up speed. It careens into the Nadders trapped in the fishing nets. The Nadders break free . . . hauling away our precious sheep.

Dad scowls furiously.

"Sorry, Dad," I say.

Fuming, my father grabs me by my collar and picks me up.

"I hit a Night Fury!" I argue. "It went down, Dad! Just off Raven Point—"

"Stop!" Dad drops me. "Do you realize what you've cost us? How do you suppose we will feed the village now?"

"I can't stop myself," I reply. "I see a dragon and I have to kill it. It's who I am, Dad."

Dad narrows his eyes. "You are many things," he growls, "but a *dragon killer* is not one of them."

CHAPTER TWO

For the rest of the day, I search Raven Point for the Night Fury I hit. By the time dusk falls, I still haven't found any sign of the dragon. "Some people lose their knife," I mutter. "I manage to lose an entire *dragon*."

I hike up a forested hill, heading toward a jagged cliff where few Vikings ever go.

At the top, I'm surprised to find snapped tree trunks. Past the broken trees is a ravine of upturned earth. I jump into the ravine and follow the torn-up ground.

I freeze. At the end of the plowed-up trail is a sleek black dragon huddled deep in the woods. It's not moving. It looks dead. I grab my dagger and approach it slowly.

The dragon is totally tangled in a bola rope. *My* bola.

"It worked," I gasp. "I did it! This fixes everything!"

Thrilled, I plant my foot on the fallen Night Fury's back leg. I raise my arms triumphantly. "*I* have brought down this mighty beast!"

The leg twitches. I jump back.

The Night Fury doesn't move, but I see the dragon staring at me. Its gaze is cold and steady. I gulp and look away, but I'm drawn back to its mesmerizing eye.

Bound by the bola rope, the dragon is defenseless. I puff myself up to my full height. "I'm going to kill you, Dragon," I announce. "I'm going to cut out your heart and take it to my father." I hold up my dagger. "I am a *Viking*!"

The Night Fury's gaze is steely, but . . . there's a

flicker of some profound emotion. It breathes raggedly, and I slump my shoulders. The dragon closes its eyes and lowers its head, accepting its fate.

I prepare to strike. My hand trembles as I stare at the dragon. It's a magnificent creature, now completely at my mercy. I inhale sharply and raise the dagger . . . but then lower it. "Oh," I groan, "who am I kidding?"

The raw wounds the rope chafed into the dragon's black hide look painful. "I did this," I mutter, ashamed.

I start to stride away. But after a few steps, I stop and glance back at the helpless beast. Making sure nobody is watching, I return to the dragon.

With my dagger, I saw through the ropes.

The Night Fury watches me cut the tangles. Finally the last loop falls free.

Instantly, the dragon pounces, knocking me to the ground. It breathes hot air into my face. We share a stare for a long, intense moment. The Night Fury roars loudly, preparing to torch me.

Then it turns and leaps into the air.

The dragon's screech echoes. It flaps its wings.

The Night Fury bashes through tree branches. It slams into a rock wall and drops off the cliff's edge, disappearing.

Breathing heavily, I stand up, weaving. I only take two steps before I crumple to the ground and pass out.

It's dark by the time I wake up and stagger back home. Dad is waiting for me, stirring the coals in the fire pit with his axe.

"We have to talk," my father says.

I nod. "I have to talk to you, too, Dad." I take a deep breath. "I've decided I don't want to fight dragons—"

"I think it's time you learn to fight dragons," Dad says. "You get your wish. You start dragon training in the morning." He holds out his giant axe.

I don't take it. "I don't want to fight dragons."

"Yes, you do," Dad counters.

"Let me say that another way," I argue. "I *can't* kill dragons."

"You will," my father replies. "It's time. This is serious, son!" He pushes the axe into my hands. "When you carry that, you carry all Vikings with you. You *think* like us. No more . . . *you*. Deal?"

I try to hold the axe up as best I can. It's incredibly heavy. "Deal," I sigh.

CHAPTER THREE

The next morning, I report for dragon training. The arena is a circular flat ring surrounded by stone walls. Gobber is our trainer. And Dad has told him to keep a careful eye on me while he's off on a dragon-finding mission. Astrid, Snotlout, Tuffnut, Ruffnut, and Fishlegs wait in the ring's center.

"The recruit who does best will win the honor of killing his first dragon in front of the entire village," Gobber informs us. He pulls a lever and a gate slides closed, shutting off the exit tunnel.

"No turning back," Astrid mutters.

I head toward the line of teenagers, lugging my axe, and stand near Astrid. "Let's get this over with," I say.

Astrid regards me dismissively. "You need to stop all of . . . ," she sneers, waving her hand from my head to my toe. "This."

"You just gestured to all of me," I say.

Behind Gobber, five doors are set into the wall. Roars of dragons echo behind each.

"Know your dragons," Gobber announces. "Gronckle, Deadly Nadder, Hideous Zippleback, Monstrous Nightmare, and Terrible Terror."

He raises the crossbeam on one door. The hinges rattle violently.

"Aren't you going to teach us first?" asks Snotlout.

Gobber opens the door. "I believe in learning on the job."

A fat Gronckle charges into the ring. I fight the urge to flee.

"Today's about survival," Gobber says as the Gronckle circles around us. "What's the first thing you need?"

"A shield!" Astrid shouts.

"Shields," Gobber confirms. "Go!"

Scattered around are shields for each of us. We rush to grab them. Ruffnut and Tuffnut grab opposite ends of a shield decorated with a skull, and squabble over it.

The Gronckle lands beside a pile of rocks and gobbles them.

"Gronckles make lava in their bellies," Gobber explains.

With a growl, the Gronckle fires a lava bomb at Tuffnut and Ruffnut. The fireball blasts the shield out of their hands, and the twins spin like tops.

"You're both out!" hollers Gobber.

The Gronckle gulps down more rocks and spews fire at Fishlegs, shattering his shield. Gobber calls Fishlegs out, and he moves to the edge of the arena, close to where I was trying to stay hidden behind a barrier.

"Hiccup, get in there!" Gobber orders. "Know your dragon's shot limit! How many shots does a Gronckle have?"

"Five!" Snotlout answers.

"No, six!" Astrid calls.

"Correct, six," Gobber says. "That's one for each of you, so watch your step."

Snotlout jumps behind Astrid, letting her face down the Gronckle. When the dragon fires, Astrid cartwheels to the side, and the explosion hits Snotlout's shield, knocking him on his butt.

"You're done!" Gobber yells at Snotlout.

Astrid stops flipping beside me behind the barrier. I grin awkwardly at her. "I guess it's just you and me."

"No," Astrid replies, "just you." She suddenly rolls away—and a fireball from the Gronckle smacks the barrier, disintegrating it. I'm totally exposed.

The Gronckle snorts and waddles toward me. I trip, and drop my shield. It rolls across the ring. I chase after it . . . catching the Gronckle's attention.

"Hiccup!" Gobber shouts.

The dragon rushes at me and pins me against the wall, smoke streaming from its nose. It opens its mouth to blast me with a lava bomb.

Gobber tackles the dragon. The Gronckle's head jerks back, and its blast hits the wall above me.

"And that's six," Gobber says in a strangled voice. He pushes the Gronckle into its cave. "Back to bed, you overgrown sausage!"

With the Gronckle locked away, I look up. There's a steaming crater in the wall.

Gobber hoists me to my feet. "Remember," he tells all of us, "a dragon will *always* go for the kill."

CHAPTER FOUR

After training, I hike to the spot in the woods where I'd seen the Night Fury. Near the torn-up ground, I find the remains of my bola, but no sign of the dragon.

I follow a trail of broken branches toward the spot where the Night Fury dropped out of sight. Near the cliff's edge, I discover an opening in the rocky wall, which reveals a natural stone passageway leading downward.

At the end of the crevasse, there's a lovely, isolated cove with a pristine pool surrounded by high stone walls.

I notice a black dragon scale by my feet. As I stoop to pick it up, I'm startled by the Night Fury swooping past me. I duck back into the crevasse.

The dragon whooshes toward the top of the cliff, flapping its wings. It loses control, slams against the cliff, and crashes onto the beach.

Then the dragon tries to climb the sheer rock wall. Its talons screech against the stone as it slips down, splashing into the pool.

It crawls toward the ocean's edge. It snaps at fish in the shallow water, but misses them. The Night Fury slumps on the beach, worn out.

"Why don't you just fly away?" I whisper.

Then I see a piece of the dragon's tail is missing. I bite my lip. That part must have gotten sheared off by my bola. I pull out my sketchbook and flip past the drawings of weapons to a blank page. I sketch the dragon quickly, desperate to record the image of this dragon with only half of a tail.

The next morning, it's back to training. Gobber lets a Deadly Nadder loose in a wooden maze. The small, spiky blue dragon chases us through the labyrinth, breathing fireworks.

"All dragons have a blind spot!" Gobber hollers. "Find it, hide in it, and strike!"

The others rush through the maze, trying to avoid the Nadder's blast by finding its blind spot.

"Get in there, Hiccup!" Gobber shouts.

That's when a row of walls collapses. Astrid comes flying through the dust and crash-lands on top of me.

"Get off of me!" Astrid yells.

"Technically, you're on me. And those skirt spikes aren't very comfy," I spew back.

Astrid untangles herself and tries to pull her axe from my shield. She plants her foot on my gut and raises both the axe and shield together. As the Nadder swoops toward us, she bashes it on the nose. It yelps and scurries away.

"Pay attention, Hiccup!" Gobber scolds me, grabbing the dragon and wrestling it back into its cave.

I look around. All eyes are on me. I dust myself off, and turn to find Astrid glaring, red-faced.

"Is there somewhere you actually belong?" she asks. "Because this isn't it."

As the sun sets, I visit the Night Fury, bringing a basket of fish.

I locate a dark alcove on the crevasse's other side. I back up, leaving the food between me and the alcove.

Finally, the Night Fury steps out. He approaches the pile of food, and sniffs it.

I take a deep breath as I get my first close-up look at the dragon. He's magnificent. His scales are glossy black from his nose to his tail, and his eyes shine like glowing emeralds. He opens his mouth, and I see empty gums.

"Huh," I mutter. "I could've sworn you had—"

With a wicked gleam, razor-sharp teeth slide out of the dragon's gums.

"Teeth," I finish, awed.

The Night Fury snatches the food and tugs it onto the beach. He chews while watching me suspiciously. The food disappears in two big gulps, and his teeth retract.

Then the dragon rushes toward me. It takes all my willpower not to flee, but I hold my ground. Barely.

"I don't have any more," I tell him.

The dragon looms over me, his green eyes glaring. He barfs up a chunk of meat at my feet. He looks at the lump, and then at me. I'm grossed out, but I grab a hunk of the regurgitated food and nibble on it, trying not to gag.

Satisfied, he almost smiles, then backs onto the beach, and blasts a circular area. When the sand glows, the dragon curls up on the hot spot. I step closer and warm my hands, noticing the dragon's damaged tail. I begin to draw designs in the sand with a twig. The dragon sees this, bites off a tree branch, and mimics my drawing. He creates a huge design in the sand around me. I walk around it and approach the dragon, holding out my hand, and I gently touch him on the nose.

CHAPTER FIVE

I build my newest invention that night in the blacksmith's shop. I heat bars of iron in the forge, and hammer them into intricate shapes on the anvil. By the break of dawn, I've built a mechanical dragon tail.

The sun is rising as I lug a basket to the cove. The Night Fury emerges from his alcove, sniffing me.

"Hey, Toothless," I say, "I brought breakfast." I dump the basket. Fish spill out. "We've got some salmon and Icelandic cod." The dragon gulps those down. "And a whole smoked eel."

Toothless chomps the eel and spits it out. He scrubs his tongue on the sand.

"Yeah," I say, "I'm not a fan, either."

While the Night Fury eats, I unwrap the metal fin. "Don't mind me," I croon. "I'll just be behind you . . . minding my own business. . . ."

I approach the injured tail, but he sweeps it away.

"It won't hurt," I say. I try to attach the fin, but he keeps moving it. "Toothless, this won't work unless you stay still!"

I drop to my knees on his tail. He tries to pull free, but I hold on. He extends his wings in protest while I fix the fin in place, tightening the straps. "Done!"

Alarmed, Toothless takes off with a snap of his wings. I grab onto his tail as I'm yanked off the ground. "No!"

I struggle to hold on as Toothless soars higher. The cove is speeding away below us. Toothless tips in the air, out of control, spinning toward a crash.

Gritting my teeth, I inch toward the folded metal fin as the dragon plummets. Right before we hit the water, I pull on the fin and it spreads like a fan. It catches the air, stabilizing the dragon.

Toothless arcs inches above the ocean, and swoops up. The dragon glances at me, his eyes glittering.

"It's working!" I scream, both excited and terrified. It's really hard to hold onto the tail and keep the fin open at the same time.

Toothless takes a sharp turn and I lose my grip. I topple off the tail and plunge into the water, screaming.

Without me to operate the fin, Toothless spins wildly. He crashes into the water like a giant cannonball.

I pop up next to the swimming dragon.

My body stings where I smacked the water, but I grin. "We *flew*."

"A Hideous Zippleback is extra tricky," Gobber explains to us as he unbars a door. "One head breathes gas, the other lights it. Know which is which!"

Two dragon heads attached by long necks to one green body jut out of the cave, peering at us. We're holding buckets of water.

"As with all dragons," Gobber continues, "you'll hear a hiss of gas before it's lit. Act quickly. A wet dragon head can't light its fire."

One Zippleback head hisses as it releases gas, and the other clicks, making sparks.

"Now!" Gobber hollers.

I hurry *toward* the Zippleback, holding my vest open.

The others can't see that I have an eel draped around my neck.

The Zippleback sniffs, disgusted, and retreats.

I hold up my hand using the eel to force the Zippleback into his cave, and I bar the door behind him. Then I close my vest before I turn around.

Everyone's gaping at me in amazement.

Except for Astrid, who's scowling suspiciously.

CHAPTER SIX

Over the next few days, I practice flying with Toothless. I become an expert at making excuses to disappear for hours.

Every evening, after flying and crashing, I make adjustments to the fin. I put together a leather harness that holds both me and the fin in place. I even invent handles and foot pedals so I can ride comfortably up on Toothless's neck.

One late afternoon, as I ride along the shoreline on Toothless, the dragon swoops toward stone sea stacks that jut from the ocean. The controls are responsive, but it's difficult to keep up with Toothless. He banks between the sea stacks, and I'm too slow with the hand controls. He bumps into a rocky formation.

"Sorry," I tell him. "My fault."

Toothless swats me with his ear, then soars upward. I see the whole of Berk below me. It's a gorgeous sight. The island looks smaller as Toothless carries me higher.

I tighten my grip on the handles. "Okay," I say nervously, "turn around now."

The temperature drops as we climb into thinner air. I can see my breath. "Stop!" I holler, gasping. "Please!"

Toothless slows down, and I exhale in relief. He stops flapping his wings, and we hang in place.

Then we drop toward the ocean far below.

In the free fall, I slip out of the harness, and float away from the dragon. "Toothless!"

Without me controlling the fin, Toothless spirals wildly. He flaps his wings, fighting to get underneath me.

I stretch out my limbs, trying to slow down. I angle toward him, diving closer.

We're falling fast now, dropping toward the ground. I kick my legs, and with a desperate stretch, I snag the harness. Just in time, I grab the controls and steer Toothless upward, missing the tops of the island's trees.

Zooming with breathtaking speed, we soar over a cliff, careening toward an obstacle course of sea stacks. With no time to think, I work the controls instinctively, making split-second turns, steering us safely through the stone towers.

Relieved and thrilled, I raise my arms and cheer.

Toothless squeals happily and spews out a fireball— in front of us.

My excitement turns to screaming horror as we fly into the fireball.

I have to smack my face to extinguish my eyebrows.

We land on a beach as the sun is setting. Then, I jump into the water, just to ensure I'm no longer on fire anywhere.

When I return to the shore, Toothless has caught a pile of fish. So I build a fire pit in the sand.

The roasting fish smell wonderful—good enough to attract a flock of Terrible Terrors. They land near the fire pit, snapping like seagulls.

One Terror hisses. He opens his mouth and releases gas, preparing to blast me.

Toothless spits a tiny flame into the Terror's mouth. The gas ignites inside the Terror, backfiring into his belly. He coughs up smoke.

I throw the blasted Terror a fish. "Not so fireproof on the inside, huh?"

As darkness falls, Toothless settles onto the sand. I lean against his belly. The stars and planets appear above and I stare into the night sky, lost in thought.

"Everything we believe about you guys is wrong," I whisper.

CHAPTER SEVEN

Later that night, Dad corners me in the blacksmith stall. "You've been keeping secrets," he accuses. "Just how long did you think you could hide it from me? So let's talk about that dragon."

"I'm so sorry," I reply quickly. "I was going to tell you. I didn't know how ..."

Dad erupts in laughter, and I stare at him in confusion.

"I was hoping for this! I just wish you would've come to me first," my father says, smiling.

I gulp in surprise. Clearly we're not talking about the same thing.

"Wait until you spill a Nadder's guts for the first time, or mount your first Gronckle

head on a spear! What a feeling!" Dad roars.

"Yeah," I say uneasily.

Dad throws his arm roughly around my shoulders. "For seventeen years, you were the worst Viking ever. I almost gave up on you! But with you doing so well in the ring, we finally have something to talk about!"

I blink at him in bewilderment. He clears his throat.

"I, um . . . brought you something," he says, his voice low. "To keep you safe in the ring. Your mother would have wanted you to have it. It's half of her breastplate."

He presents me with a horned helmet, complete with an inset ruby.

The next day, Gobber told me I was the winner of the trainees.

I swallow nervously. "So when am I ... *killing* stuff," I ask.

"Tomorrow morning," Gobber replies happily.

Later, I sneak out to the cove. I'm buckling my harness when I see Astrid sitting on a rock in the shadows.

I scream.

"What's been going on?" Astrid asks coldly. "Are you training with someone?"

Toothless lets out a growl down in the cove, and Astrid heads toward the sound.

I jump in front of her. "I've been making things!" I say, trying to distract her. "Outfits!"

Astrid grabs my hand and bends it backward.

"Ow!" I cry. "Why would you do that?"

She punches me in the arm. "That's for lying," she says. She kicks my feet out from under me and jumps on my stomach. "And that's for everything else."

After I get my breath back, Astrid has already reached the cove. I chase after her, but I can't stop her from seeing Toothless on the far end of the beach, stretching his wings.

"Get down!" Astrid shrieks, shoving me onto the sand.

Toothless bounds over to my rescue.

Astrid raises her axe.

I knock Astrid's axe to the ground. "No!"

Toothless stops short, spraying sand all over Astrid, who's frozen in shock. The dragon looks at me and then peers at Astrid, confused.

"It's okay," I say to Toothless. "She's a friend." I frown at Astrid. "You scared him."

"I scared *him*?" Astrid screeches. She lowers her voice. "Who's him?"

"Astrid, Toothless." I introduce them.

Astrid backs away toward the crevasse, her eyes wild. She bolts up the passageway.

"We're dead," I say, clambering aboard the dragon. He takes off. We catch up to Astrid in the woods, and Toothless snatches her in his talons.

"Oh, great Odin's ghost!" Astrid screams. "This is it!"

Toothless deposits Astrid on the top of the tallest pine tree. He settles on a branch sturdy enough to hold him.

Astrid dangles from the tree, kicking above the huge drop. "Get me down!"

"Give me a chance to explain," I tell her. "Just let me show you." I reach out my hand. "*Please.*"

Astrid scowls furiously, but takes my hand. I help her climb onto Toothless. Awkwardly she settles behind me on the harness. "Now get me down."

I pat Toothless's neck. "Okay," I tell the dragon. "Go."

He launches out of the tree. He hovers in the night sky momentarily, then soars upward. Then he begins a dramatic barrel roll.

Astrid clings to my back. "I'm sorry!" she yells. "Get me off this thing!"

"Wait," I say, and Toothless levels off into a cloud bank. When we burst out of the cloud cover, the gorgeous torch-lit panorama of Berk is spread beneath us. To the north, the aurora borealis shimmers with brilliant colors. Above is a milky infinity of stars. I glance at Astrid. She's grinning.

"Okay, I admit it," she says. "This is pretty cool. He's . . . amazing."

The air at the altitude of dragon flight is chilly. Astrid

rests her chin on my shoulder. I smile nervously, unsure
how to react when my dreams come true.

"So what now?" Astrid asks.

"I've been thinking a lot about dragons," I reply, "and I don't think we have to fight them. At the very least, we can get them to leave us alone."

"Hiccup," Astrid says, "your final exam is tomorrow. You're going to have to kill a dragon—"

Toothless lets out a moan.

"What's the matter?" I ask, alarmed.

Another Night Fury dives out of the clouds. It squawks at Toothless, and Toothless abruptly changes direction, swooping alongside the newcomer. We soar toward the open sea.

"What's going on?" Astrid demands.

I shake my head. "I don't know."

Other dragons appear out of the darkness, carrying sheep or fish in their talons.

"They're hauling in their kill," I guess.

Astrid squeezes me. "What does that make us?"

The dragons fall into formation, and bank east over the ocean. I've never been this far away from Berk. We fly into a red-glowing patch of clouds.

When we drop below the clouds, a massive volcano appears. Hundreds of dragon nests are tucked into nooks and crevices on the slopes.

"What my dad wouldn't give to find *this* place," I whisper.

Toothless circles the volcano and lands on a wide

ridge overlooking the caldera.

The loudest noise I've ever heard shakes the volcano. At first I think the volcano is erupting, but I realize that the deafening sound is a dragon's howl.

The dragons who brought food drop their catches into the caldera and rush away. I peer into the deep pit. Something vast squirms in the lava lake below.

"What *is* that?" Astrid whispers.

I have no idea.

A gargantuan head rises. It has six huge eyes, and dark green skin. The monster roars angrily. I don't even want to talk about its terrifying teeth.

"We gotta go, Toothless. Now," I order.

Launching into the air, Toothless heads toward Berk with a squadron of dragons returning for another raid.

Toothless lands in the cove and Astrid slides off his neck. "Let's find your dad," she says.

"Not yet!" I argue. "They'll kill Toothless. We have to think this through carefully."

Astrid crosses her arms. "We just discovered the dragons' nest. We've been searching for that since Vikings first sailed here . . . and you want to keep it a secret to protect your *pet dragon*?"

I fix her with a stare. "Yes," I reply.

Surprised by my determination, Astrid nods. "What do we do?"

"Give me until tomorrow," I say, sliding down next to her. "I'll figure this out."

"Okay," Astrid replies. She socks me in the arm. "That's for kidnapping me."

I glance at Toothless for support, but the Night Fury rolls his emerald eyes.

Astrid gives me a kiss on the cheek. "That's for everything else," she says, and she hurries out of the cove.

I rub my cheek in blissful shock.

CHAPTER EIGHT

Every Viking in Berk shows up at the arena to watch my horrifying reward for being the best trainee. I have to kill a Monstrous Nightmare—alone.

I pick up my shield and stride into the ring.

"Today my boy becomes a Viking!" Dad shouts, and the Vikings cheer.

I pick up a small pike and nod to Gobber.

Gobber opens a door. With a wicked hiss, the Monstrous Nightmare gallops into the ring. He's covered with battle scars and looks furious.

I drop my weapon and back away from

it. I extend my open palm toward the dragon. He snorts, still upset. "It's okay," I tell the Nightmare. "I'm not one of them."

The crowd murmurs, confused.

I inch closer to the Nightmare with my arms outstretched, trying to calm him. He blinks, bewildered, but seems to be relaxing.

"Start the fight!" Dad hollers as he whacks his hammer against the bars with a loud clatter.

The noise riles up the Nightmare. He snaps at me, forcing me to dodge and roll. The dragon opens his mouth to toast me.

A dark shadow falls over the arena. Toothless lands in the center of the ring.

The Vikings gasp. Dad runs to the edge of the ring, holding his hammer. Toothless locks his gaze onto the Nightmare, and the red dragon backs down. I hurry over to Toothless and stroke his muzzle.

Dad stops at the ring's edge, horrified. Vikings around him pull out weapons.

Toothless crouches, ready to defend us.

"Put your weapons away!" I yell. "He won't hurt you."

My father glares so angrily I'm surprised I don't burst into flames. "Get out of the way," he orders. He raises his hammer.

"Dad, no!" I shout.

Toothless squeezes through the fence into the stands, heading for Dad.

"Take it alive!" Dad hollers.

The Vikings swarm on top of Toothless. He flings men into the air, growling. My father bashes Toothless on his front leg, and the dragon howls. He whirls on Dad.

I hear the hiss of gas, and I scream, "Toothless—*don't*!"

I hold my breath, but there's no explosion. Toothless listened. He doesn't defend himself as Vikings pin him to the ground.

"Put it with the others!" Dad orders.

The Vikings drag Toothless to the cages.

Dad marches me into the Hall of Heroes to berate me, but he's so angry that he can't speak.

"You don't understand," I say softly. "He was protecting me."

Dad faces me, his fists clenched. He huffs in disbelief.

"He's not a killer!" I argue. "They raid us because they have to. If they don't bring back enough food, they'll be eaten themselves. There's another creature there—"

My father points a finger. "You've been to the nest? How did you find it?"

"I didn't," I reply. "Toothless did. Only a dragon can find the island."

Dad's eyebrows furrow in an expression I recognize—he has an idea.

"Dad, *no*," I say. "You don't know what you're up against. It's like nothing you've ever seen."

He strides toward the door, and I run after him and grab his arm.

"No!" I cry. "For once in your life, *will you please listen to me?*"

Dad flexes his arm, throwing me to the ground.

I stare at my father from the floor.

He wrings his hands, regretting hitting me. "You're not a Viking," he growls. "You're not my son." Then he storms out.

"Ready the ships!" he bellows to his Vikings.

I watch from a cliff as the Vikings prepare their ships. They load the vessels with catapults, weapons, and supplies.

Vikings haul Toothless onto my father's ship. He is chained to a block of wood. An iron collar has been fastened around his neck. Toothless looks absolutely miserable.

The ships set sail. As the armada pulls away, Dad stands on the bow of his vessel, glaring into the cold wind. "Lead us home, Devil!"

Astrid joins me on the cliff as the ships disappear

over the horizon. "I'm sorry," she says. "You must feel horrible. You've lost your father, your tribe, and your best friend."

"Thanks for summing that up," I reply. "Why couldn't I kill that dragon when I found him in the woods? It would have been better for everyone—even him."

Astrid nods. "The rest of us would have killed him . . . so why didn't you?"

"I couldn't!" I snap at her. "I wouldn't! I'm a coward, okay? Three hundred years and I'm the first Viking who wouldn't kill a dragon!"

"You were the first to ride one, though," Astrid says.

I look at her. "I wouldn't kill him . . . because I wanted to see what would happen next."

"So what happens next, this time?" Astrid asks.

I smile.

The other teen Vikings meet us at the dragon caves in the arena.

Fishlegs smiles. "Astrid filled us in—"

"So what insane and dangerous mission do you have in mind?" Tuffnut interrupts.

"You're crazy," Ruffnut tells me. "I like that."

"Well," I begin, "I—"

"We're in!" Snotlout cheers.

I shake my head. "You don't have to be part of this."

Astrid glares at me. "What part of 'we're in' did you miss?"

I smile, and raise the crossbeam on the Monstrous Nightmare's cage. It steps out into the center of the ring. I open my hand and slowly touch the Nightmare's muzzle. It smells me . . . and calms.

"What are you doing?" Snotlout exclaims.

"It's okay. It's okay," I reassure the group. "Now . . . stay calm and so will they."

CHAPTER NINE

hen we reach Dragon Island, the battle between the Vikings and the Red Death is under way. The monster has destroyed the ships and is spewing green fire at the Vikings. Those who have survived scurry among the volcano's rocks.

I spot Dad and Gobber running along a ridge as our squadron of dragons descends.

My father's mouth drops open when he sees us riding dragons. I'm behind Astrid on the Nadder, Snotlout rides the Nightmare, Fishlegs clings to the Gronckle, and Ruffnut and Tuffnut each perch on a head of the Zippleback.

We circle the Red Death. It's enormous, with dozens of claws, folded wings, and many eyes. My friends look terrified.

"It's still just a dragon," I yell. "Keep in its blind spot and find out if it has a shot limit. Confuse it and keep it mad. Trust your dragons! I'll be back as soon as I can."

Astrid steers the Nadder down to search for Toothless, while Snotlout aims the Nightmare into the Red Death's blind spot. I turn around to watch.

The Red Death opens its other four eyes and squints at Snotlout. Head whipping, it catches the Nightmare's wing. Snotlout tumbles onto the Red Death's head, and grabs onto an eyelid.

"It doesn't have a blind spot!" Fishlegs hollers.

As the Red Death glares at Snotlout, Ruffnut and Tuffnut swoop past on the Zippleback. Snotlout hits the monster's vast eye with his hammer, while the twins get the Zippleback to blow an explosion in the Red Death's face.

"8 . . . 9 . . . 10—!" Fishlegs shouts, counting the Red Death's blasts. "It doesn't have a shot limit! Didn't Gobber teach us anything *useful*?"

I turn back around, scanning the wrecked ships for Toothless as our Nadder dives lower. I spot Toothless, still tied to my father's burning, sinking ship. "There!" I shout.

Astrid steers us down. I hop off the Nadder and onto the ship, guarding my face from the hot flames.

"I'm good!" I call back. "Go help the others!"

As Astrid takes off, I rush over to Toothless through the flames. "It's okay, buddy," I say, releasing the muzzle. "I'm here."

Toothless screeches as I start to pull on the chains fastened to his yoke.

They won't budge. "Come on!" I shout in frustration, yanking with all my might. Suddenly the Red Death's claw swipes at Fishlegs on his Gronckle, but misses. The claw crashes onto the deck of the ship. Toothless and I are flung into the water in a barrage of burning planks and torn sails.

I desperately dive toward Toothless, who's sinking in his chains like an anchor. He's stopped struggling. I reach his chains and tug hopelessly on them, but I'm running out of air.

That's when a meaty hand closes around my arm. My father drags me toward the surface and plops me down on the shore.

"Dad," I splutter, "I—"

Without replying, my father dives back into the ocean.

He stays under the waves for a long time . . . too long. Even if my father swam all the way to the ocean floor and broke the chains around Toothless, he should be up by now.

In an explosion of foamy water, Toothless blasts out of the sea, dragging my father in his claws. He sets Dad down gently on the beach.

I climb onto Toothless's neck, but before he can take off, my father grabs my arm.

"Wait," he says.

"What?" I ask.

Dad stares into my eyes. "I'm proud to call you my son. Just . . ."

I smile at him, feeling energized by his words, but then I narrow my eyes in determination. "We're Vikings," I tell him. "It's an occupational hazard."

My father nods as Toothless launches into the air, joining the other dragons in the sky.

When Astrid spots me, she screams, "He's up! Get Snotlout out of there!"

The twins loop down and snag Snotlout off of the Red Death's eyelid. The Red Death inhales sharply, preparing to blast the Zippleback. Astrid and her Nadder get caught in the suction—and are pulled toward the monster's gaping mouth.

Toothless and I rocket down at the Red Death, and the Night Fury blasts the monster head-on. The shot distracts the Red Death enough so that its shot at Astrid is thrown off. The fireball clips the Nadder's wing.

Astrid tumbles off the Nadder. She plummets toward the ocean.

Toothless swoops down and snags Astrid's leg with his mouth. We detour briefly to drop Astrid off with the Vikings hiding in the rocks, but then soar back up at the Red Death.

"That thing has wings," I tell Toothless. "Let's see if it can use them."

CHAPTER TEN

Toothless and I streak down and circle the Red Death's snout twice before zooming upward.

As I hoped, the Red Death unfurls its massive wings and flaps them, taking off in pursuit. It picks up speed, catching up to Toothless.

"Faster than it looks, huh?" I mutter as we arc at full speed around the island with the Red Death chasing us.

When the Red Death gets close, I hear a familiar gas hiss. I lean left just as it fires. A fireball narrowly misses us. It blasts a chunk out of the volcano's slope.

"It's unstoppable," I mutter . . . and a realization strikes me. "It's unstoppable!"

It tries to incinerate us again, but I signal

for Toothless to stall, and we drop below the fireball.

The Red Death bellows in fury and rolls, diving at us.

"Come on, Toothless," I say, pointing to the clouds. "Let's even the odds."

Toothless rockets upward, surging into the clouds high above. The Red Death follows us, but immediately loses us in the dense cloud cover.

We wheel above it. Toothless spews out a blast, and punctures a hole in the monster's wing. Then we zoom away before it can fire back.

Using the clouds to hide and surprise the Red Death, we dive again and again. Toothless blasts another hole in its wings each time we break cover ... until we're down to Toothless's last shot. He squawks in frustration.

"Don't worry, buddy," I reply. "Let's make it count."

The Red Death cruises through the cloud bank, scanning for us. We burst into open air in front of its nose.

Toothless tucks in his wings, racing faster than I've ever seen him fly before. I peek back, making sure we keep ahead of the Red Death.

When the volcano appears, we pivot, diving toward the ground. The Red Death follows closely behind.

As we whiz down, Toothless weaves out of the monster's path.

"Not yet!" I scream at him. "Hold, Toothless! *Hold!*"

I tuck my head against Toothless's neck as we plummet toward the volcano. Glancing behind, I see the Red Death opening its mouth and I hear the hiss of gas.

"*Now!*" I shriek.

Toothless jackknifes in the air, so that we're suddenly facing the other direction. He belches out a fireball.

So close behind us, the Red Death swallows Toothless's blast.

The monster's six eyes widen as the gas inside it ignites. The explosion backfires down its throat, detonating through its humongous body.

"*Up*, Toothless!" I cry.

Toothless throws his wings open, pulling out of the dive, swooping upward.

Choking on the explosions, The Red Death glances up at us escaping, and back down as it plunges toward the island. The Red Death spreads its wings . . . but we have punctured too many holes.

The Red Death hits the ground headfirst.

It explodes like the end of the world.

The concussion of the blast knocks the wind out of me. I struggle to focus as pieces of the Red Death hurtle toward us. It takes everything I have to steer Toothless through the shrapnel of dragon parts. I avoid all the obstacles, just like I survived barreling between

Berk's sea stacks on one of our first flights.

I can't do anything to stop the enormous fireball expanding behind us, though—except outfly it before it swallows us.

"Faster, Toothless!" I holler.

I gasp as the Red Death's severed tail flails toward us. There's no time to react. The tail clips Toothless's, and I'm thrown from the harness, falling free. Behind me, the fireball rushes up to engulf me in flames.

Toothless brakes hard and reverses direction, diving toward me.

The last thing I see is Toothless rushing toward me as hot flames blaze all around.

Then I blindly feel us tumbling. I cling to Toothless, realizing his fireproof wings are the only thing between me and baking. We rocket down like a meteor.

WHAM!

We wallop the ground. The pain of our crash is so intense that I black out.

I awake alone in my bed.

One of my legs is itching horribly, and I raise my blanket to take a peek.

I inhale sharply in shock. The lower part of my right leg looks very different.

I don't know if my dragon is even alive. Swinging

out of bed, I hobble toward the front door.

As soon as I open the door, I spot a Monstrous Nightmare flying toward me. I brace myself for a fiery attack . . . which never comes.

The Nightmare banks overhead, and soars away to land in a field near cheering children. I blink, unable to believe my eyes.

All over town, Vikings and dragons are getting along. Nadders and Zipplebacks bask on the rooftops. There isn't an axe in sight.

A Gronckle lands nearby, carrying a tree trunk in his mouth. He shows a Viking what he's found. The warrior pats his head.

I take a step outside and find my father waiting for me. "I knew it," I mutter. "I'm dead."

Dad laughs. "No, but you gave it your best shot!"

"What do you think?" he asks.

All I can do is shrug in amazement.

"Turns out all we needed was a little more of . . ." Dad waves his hand at me from head to toe. "*This*."

I laugh. "You just gestured to all of me." My laugh cuts off abruptly. "But where's Toothless? Is he—"

Before I can panic, I see Astrid leading Toothless toward us. My dragon has a brand-new saddle and tail. He bounces excitedly as I hurry over.

"I'm excited to see you too, bud," I tell my dragon.

Astrid hops off Toothless and quickly jabs me in the arm. "That's for scaring me."

I groan and rub my arm. "Is it always going to be this way?" I ask. "Because I—"

Astrid grabs my shoulders with her strong hands and plants an intense kiss right on my mouth.

"I could get used to it," I finish, grinning dopily.

With Astrid's arm draped over my shoulder, I stare out at our transformed village. Fishlegs is washing his Gronckle. Snotlout streaks past on his Monstrous Nightmare, leading a group of new riders on multicolored dragons.

Astrid steps away, and I climb onto Toothless's neck. I slide my foot into the stirrup—when I'm on Toothless, I'm whole again.

After climbing aboard her Nadder, Astrid smiles at me and takes off.

This is Berk.

The best part is the pets. While other places have ponies or parrots, we have . . . *dragons*.

Toothless snorts and launches into the sky. We swoop around other Vikings riding dragons, and soar out over the churning ocean waves gleaming in the sunshine.